The

Sandwalk

Adventures

AN ADVENTURE IN EVOLUTION
TOLD IN FIVE CHAPTERS

BY

JAY HOSLER

The world shall perish not for lack of wonders,
but for lack of wonder.

-J.B.S. Haldane

For Jack

Also By Jay Hosler
Clan Apis

The Sandwalk Adventures

First edition

Printed in Canada

ISBN: 0-9677255-1-8

an Active Synapse production

Active Synapse
4258 North High Street
Columbus OH 43214-3048
Fax (614) 882-8470
www.ActiveSynapse.com
info@ActiveSynapse.com

Active Synapse
Probably Good For Your Brain!

CONTENTS

Chapter One
GOD'S FOLLICLE

BUT, SINCE NO ONE HAD ANY BETTER IDEAS, THEY DID AS FLYCATCHER SUGGESTED.

"THIS SHOULD BE VERY ENTERTAINING," THEY LAUGHED.

USING ALL OF THEIR GODLY POWERS, THEY GAVE THE SHIP A MIGHTY SHAKE.

WITHIN MINUTES, FLYCATCHER FELT THE OCEAN STIR INSIDE HIM.

IT GURGLED AND SWIRLED DEEP IN HIS BELLY.

HIS KNEES WENT WEAK AS THE WATERS ROARED UP HIS THROAT AND SLAMMED AGAINST HIS TEETH.

THEN HE OPENED HIS MOUTH---

18

LA-LA-LA-LAA

WILLY!

I BETTER GET A MOP.

AAAAA oomp!

CUT IT OUT!

...c-cut...?

WHO'S THERE?

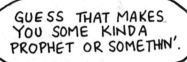

GUESS THAT MAKES YOU SOME KINDA PROPHET OR SOMETHIN'.

SHUT-UP!

TOLD YA.

HE HEARD YOU. NOT ME.

SHUT-UP?

I'M SORRY, SIR. I WASN'T TALKING TO YOU.

WELL, WHAT A RELIEF. I'M HEARING VOICES BUT THEY AREN'T TALKING TO ME.

TSK. MOM SAID WE'RE NOT SUPPOSED TO SAY THAT.

...oh, dear, that's no relief at all...

20

I DON'T KNOW HOW, BUT YOU CAN HEAR ME AND I HAVE A BUNCH OF QUESTIONS.

WHO ARE YOU?

IT'S ME, SIR.

MARA

I'M ONE OF YOUR CREATURES.

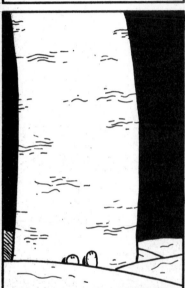

you're confusing him again.

I'M SORRY, SIR.

I KNOW I'M JUST A LOWLY MITE LIVING IN YOUR EYEBROW, BUT I WAS KINDA HOPING YOU WOULD TALK TO ME FOR A LITTLE WHILE.

YOU'RE IN MY EYEBROW?

25

Chapter Two
THE STONE PATH

T-T-T-TODAY'S S-S-S-STORY IS... ...uh.... ABOUT WHEN F-F-FLY-CATCHER BATTLED... B-BATTLED T-T-T-THE...uh... THINGEE...

...A-A-AND...um... HE WON!

the end

GO, FLYCATCHER! WOO!

41

HEY, WHEN YOU GET A CHANCE, TELL HIM THAT SO FAR THIS STORY **STINKS.**

ALTHOUGH I DIDN'T KNOW IT AT THE TIME, I GUESS YOU COULD SAY HE GAVE ME THE "GIFT" OF TIME AND HELPED PAVE THE WAY FOR MY UNDERSTANDING OF HOW THE WORLD WORKS.

DID HE **ACTUALLY** PAVE THE WAY, CREATING THE **LEGENDARY SMOOTH STONE PATH OF UNDERSTANDING?**

No

HE JUST HELPED ME TO BROADEN MY HORIZONS.

hmm.

thrilling.

IT WAS!

HE HAD LEARNED AN **ANCIENT** TRUTH ABOUT THE EARTH.

THROUGH THE DEVINE REVELATION OF THE **MYTHIC MANTLE?**

THROUGH HARD WORK AND STUDY.

WOULD YOU LET ME TELL THIS STORY?

yes, sir.

LYELL LEARNED THE EARTH WAS OLDER THAN ANYONE HAD EVER THOUGHT. IN FACT, HE CONSIDERED IT UNIMAGINABLY OLD!

WHO CARES?

ASK HIM WHO CARES.

WILLY WOULD LIKE TO KNOW HOW THE EARTH'S AGE IS RELEVANT TO HOW LIFE IS SHAPED, SIR.

HEY! THAT'S NOT WHAT I SAID!

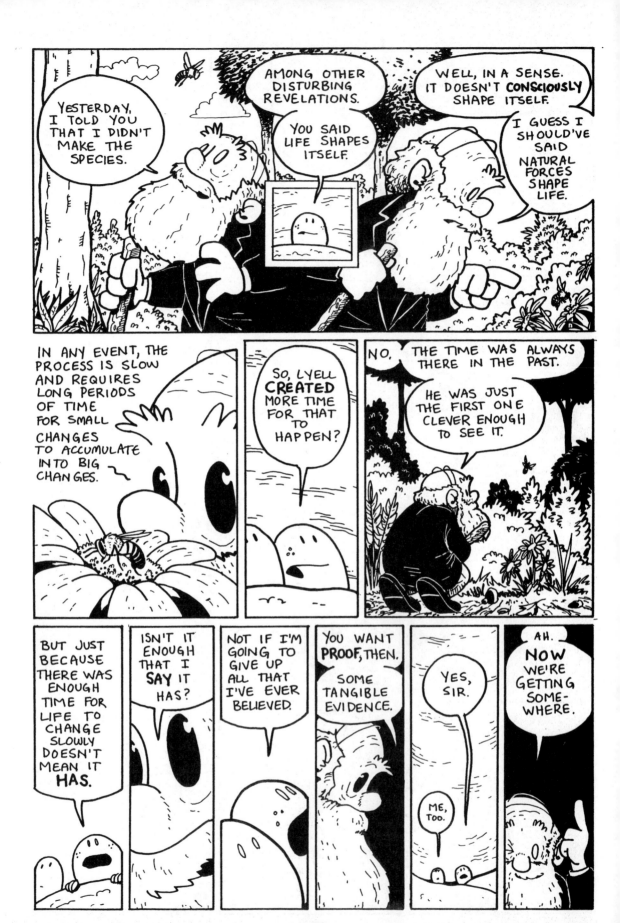

WE HAD BEEN SAILING ALONG THE EASTERN COAST OF SOUTH AMERICA AND OUR TRIP WAS DELAYED IN MONTEVIDEO.

WHILE OUR CAPTAIN BUSIED HIMSELF CHECKING AND RECHECKING HIS CHARTS...

... I PACKED THE MANY SPECIMENS I HAD MOST RECENTLY COLLECTED. (I HAD TO SEND THEM BACK TO SCIENTISTS IN ENGLAND, YOU SEE.)

I FILLED TWO BOXES AND A CASK WITH BIRD AND ANIMAL SKINS, A JAR OF FISHES, A COLLECTION OF MICE, A CASE OF INSECTS AND A BOX OF STONES.

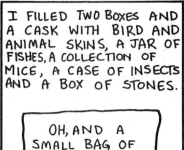

OH, AND A SMALL BAG OF SEEDS.

(I WAS TERRIBLY IDLE IN BOTANY)

BUT THE PLEASURE OF PACKING A COLLECTION **PALES** IN COMPARISON TO THE **THRILL** OF ACTUALLY **COLLECTING** IT. I SOON GREW RESTLESS TO ADD TO MY TREASURES.

THERE WAS ONE PLACE IN PARTICULAR THAT FIRED MY IMAGINATION.

I HAD MISSED AN OPPORTUNITY TO VISIT IT EARLIER IN THE VOYAGE BECAUSE I HAD FALLEN ILL.

BUT NOW THAT MY HEALTH WAS SOUND, I OUTFITTED A SMALL EXPEDITION TO THE VILLAGE OF **MERCEDES** ON THE RIO URUGUAY AND INTO THE LAND OF THE GIANT SLOTHS!

ALL RIGHT! GIANT SLOTHS!

WAS IT DANGEROUS?

YES, BUT THE GAUCHOS IN OUR PARTY WERE BRAVE AND NOBLE GUIDES. AND FORTUNATELY, THE ROUTE WE TOOK WAS WELL POPULATED SO WE DIDN'T ENCOUNTER ANY ROBBERS.

THERE WAS SOME EXCITEMENT ON THE SECOND DAY WHEN OUR WAY WAS BLOCKED BY THREE FLOODED STREAMS. SINCE THERE WAS NO GOING AROUND OR GOING BACK, WE HAD TO CROSS IN BOATS AND ON HORSEBACK.

A FEW DAYS LATER, OUTSIDE THE VILLAGE OF LAS VACAS, WE CAME ACROSS FRESH TRACKS.

OOOOO

BUT THEY WERE ONLY THOSE OF A JAGUAR AND, DESPITE A SEARCH OF NEARBY TREES, WE NEVER ACTUALLY SAW IT.

aww.

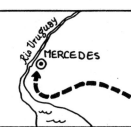

WE CONTINUED ON TO MERCEDES...

URUGUAY

ARGENTINA

MERCEDES

Rio Uruguay

... WHERE WE STAYED AT THE HOME OF A GENTLEMAN NAMED KEANE.

OUR HOST KNEW THE AREA WELL AND TOLD ME OF A FARM NEARBY THAT HAD GIANT'S BONES LYING ABOUT THE YARD.

NO DOUBT THE SCATTERED REMAINS OF THE GIANT SLOTH'S VICTIMS!

oh, baby, this was worth the wait.

FOUR DAYS LATER, WE RODE TO A FARMHOUSE ON THE SARANDIS AND PAID THE FARMER 18 PENCE TO ENTER HIS LAND.

GRACIAS.

WITHIN MOMENTS, I CAME FACE TO FACE WITH MY QUARRY.

AAAAAHH! GIANT SLOTH!

DID YOU SLAY IT QUICKLY, SIR? OR WAS THERE AN EPIC STRUGGLE?

EPIC STRUGGLE! EPIC STRUGGLE!

WHAT ARE YOU...?

50

AND, IT WASN'T ACTUALLY A GIANT SLOTH (although we did find several sloth bones). NO, THE 18-PENCE SKULL BELONGED TO ANOTHER LARGE MAMMAL THAT HAD LIVED AT THE SAME TIME AS THE GIANT SLOTHS.

SIR RICHARD OWEN ANALYZED THE SKULL A FEW YEARS AFTER I FOUND IT.

HE NAMED THE BEAST **TOXODON.**

AND IT WAS **ALREADY** DEAD?

ITS ENTIRE SPECIES HAD BEEN EXTINCT FOR 15,000 YEARS.

OH, YES.

i see.

IT WAS A LUCKY FIND, REALLY.

THE SKULL HAD BEEN EXPOSED WHEN A FLOOD WASHED AWAY PART OF A BANK OF EARTH. UNFORTUNATELY, A FEW LOCAL BOYS HAD USED IT FOR TARGET PRACTICE AND KNOCKED ALL OF ITS TEETH OUT.

STILL, THE SKULL WAS OTHERWISE INTACT AND I FOUND A TOOTH LATER THAT FIT IT PERFECTLY.

SO, DESPITE THE FACT THAT IT WAS OVER TWO FEET LONG, I WAS SO DELIGHTED WITH THE SKULL THAT I RODE THE ENTIRE 120 MILES BACK TO MONTEVIDEO WITH IT ON MY LAP.

THE END.

WHOA.

THAT STORY JUST GOT **WORSE** AND WORSE.

SO, JUST TO CLARIFY, SIR: THE TOXODON WAS ALREADY EXTINCT?

YES.

AND THE SLOTHS, TOO?

THAT'S THE WHOLE POINT, MARA. THESE ANIMALS NO LONGER EXIST.

AH.

IN THAT CASE, I FEEL COMPELLED TO TELL YOU THAT YOUR STORY NEEDS WORK.

NOT ENOUGH MYSTICAL VOMITING?

NO PEBBLE OF PERCEPTION

NO MYTHIC MANTLE.

NO SMOOTH STONE PATH OF UNDERSTANDING

AND THE MONSTER HAD ALREADY EXPIRED.

YOU'VE MISSED THE POINT ENTIRELY.

WHAT POINT?

THE MOST EXCITING THING YOU DID WAS PICK THINGS UP.

BAH! WHY DO YOU FEEL COMPELLED TO DRAPE THE ELEGANT WONDERS OF NATURE IN A GAUDY GOWN OF MUMBO-JUMBO, MARA?

STILL, YOU WERE A LITTLE WORDY THERE FOR AWHILE.

I'LL TRY TO DO BETTER TOMORROW.

I'M GOING IN FOR LUNCH NOW.

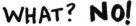

WHAT? **NO!** YOU STILL HAVEN'T TOLD US **HOW** LIFE CHANGES!

I GUESS I HAVEN'T

BUT, YOU NEEDED TO KNOW THIS STUFF BEFORE WE GO ANY FURTHER.

HOW CAN WAIT UNTIL TOMORROW.

BUT YOU SAID YOU'D TELL US **TODAY**.

YOU'RE **THAT** ANXIOUS TO KNOW MORE?

YES!

INTERESTING. YOU REALIZE WHAT THIS MEANS, DON'T YOU?

NO.

WHAT?

Chapter Three
DARWIN SAVES THE WORLD

HE HAD A COUGHING FIT AND COLLAPSED DURING HIS WALK.

MY WORD.

FORTUNATELY, JACKSON WAS NEARBY AND HEARD POLLY BARKING.

FORTUNATE, INDEED.

THERE ARE TIMES WHEN I THINK THAT SANDWALK WILL KILL HIM, FRANCIS.

OH, MOTHER...

I DO.

THIS THEORY OF HIS HAS CONSUMED HIS **THOUGHTS** FOR DECADES.

IN THE PROCESS, I BELIEVE IT HAS CONSUMED HIS **HEALTH**, AS WELL.

AND NOWHERE HAS HIS THEORY CONSUMED MORE OF **BOTH**...

...THAN ON THAT PATH.

ARE YOU READY FOR THIS, MARA?

I GOTTA BE. HE RISKED HIS HEALTH TO TELL US **HOW** LIFE IS SHAPED AND COLLAPSED IN THE PROCESS.

THE LEAST I CAN DO IS TELL HIS STORY.

MOM! MARA WANTS TO TELL A **NEW** STORY!

MARA, THERE HASN'T BEEN A NEW STORY FOR GENERATIONS. THE OLD ONES HAVE ALWAYS BEEN MORE THAN ENOUGH FOR US.

YES, MA'AM, BUT... THIS IS A REALLY **GOOD** STORY.

IT **IS**, MOM. I HEARD IT.

IS THAT SO, WILLY?

WELL, THEN, YOU BETTER TELL IT, MARA.

THANKS, MOM

GO AHEAD, SIS. I'M RIGHT BEHIND YOU.

OK, SO LIKE I SAID, THIS STORY TAKES PLACE ON THE SANDWALK.

WALK OF WONDERS.

sigh.

walk of wonders.

AFTER HIS TIME ON THE GREAT SHIP, FLYCATCHER SPENT MANY YEARS ON THE WALK OF WONDERS PONDERING THE ORIGIN OF THE SPECIES. HE MARKED HIS TIME ON THESE STROLLS WITH A SIMPLE TRADITION.

HE LIKED TO LINE UP SMALL STONES ACROSS THE PATH AND KICK ONE OUT OF PLACE EVERY TIME HE COMPLETED A CIRCUIT ON THE SANDWALK.

SMALL STONES?

THAT'S NOT VERY GODLY.

OK, **BOULDERS** THEN!

OOOF!

MARA....

WHAT? THEY'RE BOULDERS TO **US**, WILLY.

ANYWAY, ONE DAY FLYCATCHER SAID:

I'VE SPENT MUCH OF MY ADULT LIFE THINKING ABOUT **HOW** LIFE IS SHAPED, MARA.

I'VE COMPLETED INNUMERABLE CIRCUITS ON THIS PATH.

AND I'VE KICKED A **LOT** OF THESE STONES.

I'M SURE THEY HAD IT COMING, SIR.

WAAAIT A MINUTE.

YOU CAN TALK TO FLYCATCHER IN THIS STORY?

IT'S A **FANTASY EPIC!**

WOULD YOU GUYS PIPE DOWN AND LET HER TELL THE STORY?

ALL RIGHT, ALL RIGHT...

FLYCATCHER'S QUEST TO UNDERSTAND **HOW** LIFE IS SHAPED LASTED SEVERAL YEARS.

IT BEGAN WITH SOMETHING HE HAD NOTICED DURING HIS TIME ON THE **GREAT SHIP...**

WE'RE ALL DIFFERENT, MARA.

...uh...

YES, SIR.

YOU'RE MUCH TALLER THAN I AM.

YES, WELL, THAT'S NOT QUITE WHAT I MEANT.

ONE OF THE THINGS I NOTICED DURING MY TRAVELS WAS THAT EVEN THOUGH ORGANISMS OF THE SAME SPECIES LOOK VERY SIMILAR, THEY ARE NOT IDENTICAL.

THERE ARE SLIGHT VARIATIONS IN THE FEATURES OF ALL CREATURES.

NOT IN US!

WE MITES ARE AAAALLL THE SAME.

THAT'S RIGHT!

SCHMACK

REALLY? THEN HOW DO YOU KNOW WHEN YOU'RE TALKING TO WILLY?

WELL, WILLY DOESN'T HAVE FRECKLES LIKE I...

...oh...

...please continue...

THAT OBSERVATION EVENTUALLY BECAME MY FIRST POSTULATE FOR HOW LIFE IS SHAPED:

INDIVIDUALS WITHIN SPECIES ARE VARIABLE.

TOK!

WELL, THEN YOUR SPECIES USES AN UNWISE REPRODUCTIVE STRATEGY. INBREEDING COULD MAKE YOUR OFFSPRING WEAK AND SICKLY.

BUT..

YOU MARRIED YOUR COUSIN.

COUGH cough COUGH cough cough

that's :cough: different. my prospects were... limited by the strictly proscribed nature of my social class.....

MORE LIMITED THAN SOLITARY CONFINEMENT IN A HAIR FOLLICLE?

COUGH!

HEY, IS THE SKIN AROUND HERE GETTING WARMER?

AND PINKER.

THIS SKIN IS DEFINITELY PINKER

I THINK HE'S BLUSHING.

I AM NOT!

cough

YOU'VE DISTRACTED ME.

cough cough

YOU WERE TALKING ABOUT YOU-KNOW-WHAT..

OH, YES, MY SECOND POSTULATE FOR HOW LIFE IS SHAPED:

70

76

KIDS?

WELL...uh.... **NO**, NOT EXACTLY. MY WIVES WANT THEM, BUT I WANTED TO FOCUS ON MY CAREER FOR AWHILE.

WELL, IN **THAT** CASE, KOR-GUU...

...I WIN.

WHAT?

WHAT MANNER OF TRICKERY IS **THIS**?

NO TRICK. I MAY BE AN OLD FELLOW, BUT I'VE HAD SEVERAL CHILDREN.

EVOLUTIONARY FITNESS ISN'T A MEASURE OF PHYSICAL PROWESS, YOU CHITINOUS CRETIN.

IT'S AN INDEX OF REPRODUCTIVE SUCCESS.

hmm

RELAX, DEAR.

IN FACT, UNTIL WE HEAR THE PITTER-PATTER OF BABY KOR-GUUS, YOUR FITNESS WILL REMAIN A BIG, FAT **ZERO**.

ZERO?

I GOTTA GET HOME....

DEFEATED AND DEJECTED, THE GIANT PURPLE SPACE BEETLES LEFT. AS THEY DID, FLYCATCHER STOOD ON HIS SANDWALK AND SHARED THE VICTORY WITH HIS FAITHFUL COMPANION.

GOOD THING HE DIDN'T WANT TO ARM WRESTLE!

INDEED. HE WOULD HAVE HAD A **LEG** UP ON YOU, OLD FRIEND!

HAHAHAHA!

BUT NO SOONER HAD KOR-GUU LEFT THAN THE STRAIN OF THE CONFLICT **OVERWHELMED** OUR HERO.

Cough cough

...get help... cough

...old girl...

RUFF RUFF RUFF RUFF!

WHAT HAPPENED **THEN?**

I DON'T KNOW YET.

A CLIFFHANGER?

NO FAIR!

SORRY.

STILL, IT WAS COOL HOW FLYCATCHER USED THAT FITNESS-THING AGAINST THAT BIG DOPE KOR-GUU.

THAT'S SORTA THE TAKE-HOME MESSAGE.

LIFE IS SHAPED BY THOSE THAT PASS ON THEIR TRAITS TO THE NEXT GENERATION.

IF YOU REMEMBER ONLY **ONE** THING, REMEMBER **THAT.**

HEH.

NOT BAD.

NOT THE WAY **I** WOULD HAVE DONE IT, MIND YOU.

Chapter Four
THE APPLICATION OF PRESSURE

THUNDER ECHOED THROUGH THE LAND
AS THE FEROCIOUS BATTLE NEARED
ITS CONCLUSION.

FLYCATCHER'S FISTS RAINED DOWN UPON
THE BARBARIC BEETLE IN A FLURRY OF FURY.

AS THE GREAT DARK INSECT
FELT HIS CHITINOUS EXOSKELETON
BEGIN TO BUCKLE, HE
WHIMPERED FOR
MERCY.

...please...
...stop....

83

AND JUST THAT QUICKLY, THE BATTLE WAS OVER.

AS THE DUST SETTLED, THE SCENE SHIFTED FROM HOSTILITY TO HEALING.

FLYCATCHER BEGAN TO GLOW.

TWIN BEAMS OF PURE LIGHT LEPT FORTH FROM HIS EYES.

THEIR SHIMMERING ENERGIES ENVELOPED THE FALLEN INSECT AND INSTANTLY MENDED HIS WOUNDS.

LET THAT BE A LESSON TO YOU, KOR-GUU. NOW **GO,** AND DO NOT ANGER ME AGAIN.

AND WITH THAT, FLYCATCHER TOOK HIS LEAVE.

BUT A CLEAR VIEW OF FLYCATCHER'S BACK WAS ALL THE INCENTIVE THE COWARDLY COLEOPTERAN NEEDED TO **STRIKE!**

FOOL! OUR SWARMS SHALL BLACKEN YOUR SKIES!

NEVER!

IN THE BLINK OF AN EYE, FLYCATCHER HAD KOR-GUU IN HIS CLUTCHES.

YOU ASKED FOR THIS.

IS IT TOO LATE TO ASK FOR SOMETHING ELSE?

89

OH, MIGHTY FLY CATCHER, DELIVER US!

WE BESEECH THEE!

FORGIVE OUR DOUBT!

WE BELIEVE!

WE BELIEVE!

oh, not this again...

WHAT DO YOU WANT?

IT'S JUST ME, OH MIGHTY ONE, LITTLE MARA, YOUR FAITHFUL SERVANT.

ugh. I THOUGHT WE WERE DONE.

DIDN'T I EXPLAIN THE BASICS OF EVOLUTION TO YOU?

YES, YOUR MAJESTY.

BUT I NOW SEE WHAT YOU WERE REALLY DOING.

THIS SHOULD BE GOOD...

IT WAS A TEST!

WHEN YOU SAID THE WORLD WASN'T 58 YEARS OLD AND THAT YOU DIDN'T CREATE THE SPECIES, YOU WERE TESTING OUR FAITH!

OH, FOR HEAVEN'S SAKE...

AND WE FAILED!

OH, HOW WE FAILED!

SHE FAILED MORE THAN I DID, SIR.

sigh.

CHARLES!

WHERE DO YOU THINK YOU'RE GOING?

IT'S TIME FOR MY WALK, EMMA.

BUT, YOU'RE IN NO CONDITION...

DEAR, I'VE BEEN IN "NO CONDITION" MOST OF MY ADULT LIFE.

BUT...

IT'S NOON. MY SANDWALK IS CALLING.

YOU...

I WON'T BE LONG.

HELLO? CAN WE GET ON WITH THIS?

NO.

NO.

INDIVIDUALS DON'T EVOLVE, MARA.

NATURAL SELECTION PICKS INDIVIDUALS FOR SURVIVAL, **BUT** IT'S **POPULATIONS** THAT CHANGE AND EVOLVE OVER TIME.

WE NEED TO EVOLVE SOME WINGS, **PRONTO!**

NO.

THAT'S NOT FAIR!

IT'S A **STRUGGLE** FOR SURVIVAL, MARA.

I NEVER SAID IT WAS FAIR.

FINE!

BUT, IF THERE'S GONNA BE A STRUGGLE, AT LEAST TELL US HOW TO FIGHT THIS ZIT!

IT MAY SURPRISE YOU TO LEARN THAT MY EXPERIENCE IN SUCH MATTERS IS SOMEWHAT LIMITED.

C'MON!

HOW ARE WE SUPPOSED TO SURVIVE A STRUGGLE IF WE DON'T HAVE THE MEANS TO DO BATTLE?!?

YOUR **MEANS** ARE THE TRAITS YOU HAVE AND THE VARIATIONS THEREIN.

huh?

SPRECHEN SIE ENGLISH?

I DON'T UNDERSTAND, SIR.

YOU MAY SURVIVE IF YOU HAVE A VARIATION THAT GIVES YOU AN ADVANTAGE OVER THE PIMPLE.

I CAN'T BELIEVE I JUST **SAID** THAT.

NOW WE'RE GETTING SOMEWHERE!

WILLY AND I HAVE **PLENTY** OF TRAITS AND VARIATIONS!

ANYTHING USEFUL?

WE'RE KINDA BULLET-SHAPED.

JET PROPULSION?

SOME ANIMALS CAN DO THAT.

OK, THIS IS GOOD. THIS IS **VERY** GOOD. **FIRST**, WE APPLY PRESSURE TO THE AMMONIA CRYSTALS STORED IN OUR ABDOMENS.

THEN, WHEN WE REACH MAXIMUM PRESSURE, WE PROPEL OURSELVES TO SAFETY BY EXPLOSIVELY RELEASING THE CRYSTALS FROM OUR⋯

..butts..

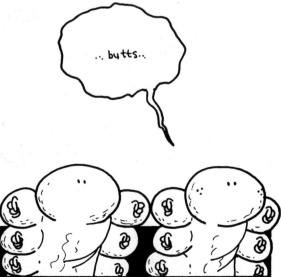

OOOO, I **KNEW** NOT HAVING BUTTS WOULD COME BACK AND BITE US IN THE---

BUTTS?

WHICH WE DON'T HAVE!

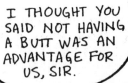

I THOUGHT YOU SAID NOT HAVING A BUTT WAS AN ADVANTAGE FOR US, SIR.

I'M SURE IT HAS BEEN.

BUT AN ADVANTAGE UNDER ONE SET OF CONDITIONS CAN BECOME A DISADVANTAGE IF THE CONDITIONS CHANGE.

THERE'S NO WAY TO KNOW IN ADVANCE IF WE'LL SURVIVE?

I'M AFRAID NOT.

SO, THIS ISN'T A TEST OF FAITH...

...IT'S AN EXPERIMENT!

WHAT?

BUT HOW?

A LITTLE BUMP OF TISSUE GRADUALLY GOT BIGGER WITH EACH GENERATION UNTIL IT WAS A WING, BLAH, BLAH, BLAH...

WHAT ADVANTAGE WOULD A LITTLE BUMP BE FOR FLIGHT?

...huh...?

well...

...NONE AT FIRST, I GUESS.

SO, HOW COULD NATURE SELECT FOR A WING IF THE FIRST LITTLE BUMP WAS **USELESS** FOR FLIGHT?

I... ...uh..

WHAT IF THE WING STARTED AS SOMETHING ELSE?

WHAT IF THAT LITTLE BUMP WAS A GILL USED TO BREATHE?

COULD IT BE ADVANTAGEOUS FOR THE **GILL** TO GET BIGGER?

SURE. THE INSECT COULD GET MORE AIR THAT WAY.

WHAT IF THE GILL GOT BIG ENOUGH TO USE FOR GLIDING?

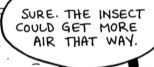

THEN NATURAL SELECTION COULD START WORKING ON IT AS A WING!

AN INTERESTING STEP SIDEWAYS, WOULDN'T YOU AGREE?

THAT'S IT! WE'LL SHIFT THE FUNCTION OF ONE OF OUR TRAITS TO ESCAPE!

NOW WAIT, THAT'S NOT...

WELL, WE BETTER HURRY! THE SINGING IS GETTING **LOUDER!**

START LOOKING FOR SOMETHING ON OUR BODIES THAT COULD BE USED LIKE A WING!

I'M LOOKIN', BUT THERE'S NOT THAT **MUCH** OF ME!

OUR ARMS!

OF COURSE! WHO NEEDS **EIGHT** ARMS?

NOT ME!

START FLAPPIN'!

INDIVIDUALS

FLAP	FLAP
FLAP	FLAP
FLAP	FLAP
FLAP	FLAP
FLAP	FLAP
FLAP	FLAP

DON'T

FLAP	FLAP
FLAP	
FLAP	FLAP
FLAP	
FLAP	FLAP
FLAP	

EVOLVE,

FLAP
FLAP
FLAP
FLAP
FLAP
FLAP

MARA.

GAH!

STOP LAUGHING AT US!

SHE'S GONNA BLOW!

101

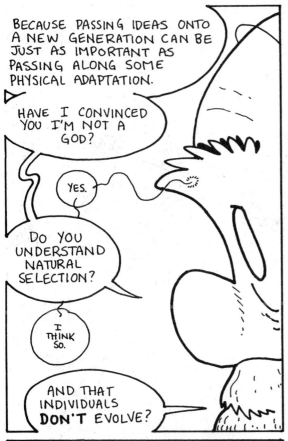

BECAUSE PASSING IDEAS ONTO A NEW GENERATION CAN BE JUST AS IMPORTANT AS PASSING ALONG SOME PHYSICAL ADAPTATION.

HAVE I CONVINCED YOU I'M NOT A GOD?

YES.

DO YOU UNDERSTAND NATURAL SELECTION?

I THINK SO.

AND THAT INDIVIDUALS **DON'T** EVOLVE?

YES, SIR.

GOOD. I WANT YOU TO SPREAD THE WORD.

WHAT?

GO DISPEL THE MYTHS ABOUT ME.

WHA--? YOU WANT **ME** TO DO THAT?

YES.

YOU ARE PICKING **ME**?

YES. YES. OBVIOUSLY!

I'M SORRY, SIR. I JUST WANTED TO CLARIFY MY ROLE IN ALL OF THIS.

AND HAVE YOU?

I BELIEVE SO...

Chapter Five
LEGACY

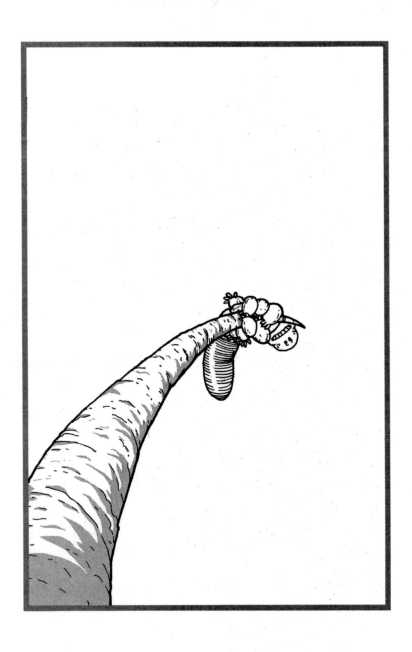

GEE, CAMPBELL, IT'S ONLY FOUR SYLLABLES.

THE CHO SEN ONE.

OH, BROTHER.

IS FLYCATCHER TALKING TO YOU AGAIN, MARA?

DID HE TELL YOU TO GO FORTH AND BE ANNOYING?

HEY, YOU GUYS SHOULD LISTEN TO HER.

SURE! ANYTHING FOR A LAUGH!

HA HA HA

I AM THE CHOSEN ONE!

NO, YOU ARE A LOUSY STORYTELLER DESPERATE FOR ATTENTION.

WELL, AT LEAST MY STORIES ARE TRUE.

EXCUSE ME?

YOU HEARD ME.

ARE YOU SUGGESTING OUR STORIES AREN'T TRUE?

YES.

OUR STORIES ARE THE VERY FOUNDATION OF WHO WE ARE, MARA!

WELL, THAT EXPLAINS WHY YOU'RE SUCH A FLAKE!

WHY YOU!

WHAT ARE YOU DOING?

SPREADING THE WORD, WILLY.

YOU'RE BEING A JERK.

CAMPBELL AND I ALWAYS TALK TO EACH OTHER THIS WAY!

YEAH, WELL, OTHERS ARE LISTENING.

SIGH.

O.K.

I'M SORRY, CAMPBELL.

OK.

DIMWIT,

ooo, yeah, I'm sorry, all right...

SORRY YOU'RE SUCH A COLOSSAL IGNORAMUS!

THAT'S IT!

YER GONNA GET IT!

OH, WHAT ARE YOU GONNA DO, MIGHTY MITE? RUN WILLY AND ME OUT OF TOWN?

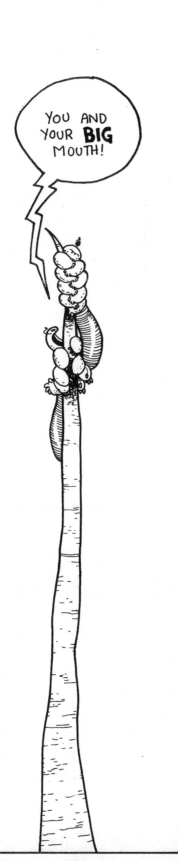

YOU AND YOUR **BIG** MOUTH!

NICE ONE, CAMPBELL.

WHAT'S GOING ON HERE?

MOM!

WELL?

NUTHIN'?

NOTHING? WHAT ARE WILLY AND MARA DOING UP THERE?

HANGIN' OUT?

109

110

WHAT'S THIS LAST QUESTION?

HOW ARE WE MADE?

I DON'T KNOW.

GOOD-BY.

THAT'S IT?

YES. NOW LEAVE ME ALONE.

BUT...

I DON'T WANT TO TALK ABOUT IT.

WELL I DO!

MY FAMILY IS WATCHING AND THIS IS MY CHANCE TO PROVE I'M NOT SOME KINDA NUT!

I CAN'T HELP YOU.

GIVE ME SOMETHING.

I HAVE NOTHING TO GIVE.

BUT...

I DON'T WANT TO TALK ABOUT IT, MARA!

SO, THAT'S IT, HUH?

YES.

114

FINE. WE ALREADY HAVE A GOOD EXPLANATION FOR THE PROCESS, ANYWAY.

I'M SURE YOU DO.

YOU'LL **LOVE** THIS.

WE BELIEVE THAT FLYCATCHER— THAT'S YOU, **YOUR WORSHIP**— CREATES A FOLLICLE MITE BY REACHING INTO THE MOTHER AND REMOVING A FIBER OF HER BEING AND THEN DOING THE SAME TO THE FATHER.

FLYCATCHER THEN USES HIS MIGHTY FINGERS TO TWIST THE TWO FIBERS TOGETHER.

AND FINALLY, HE WEAVES A NEW MITE FROM THE DOUBLE-STRAND OF THREAD.

I THINK THAT STORY IS A **BEAUT,** DON'T YOU SIR?

ridiculous.

THEY CHASED ME OUT OF THE FOLLICLE AND UP THIS HAIR, Y'KNOW!

WELL, I'M...

I QUITE LITERALLY GOT THE SHAFT BECAUSE OF YOU!

I...

I CAN'T BELIEVE I TOOK A SHOT IN THE EYE FOR YOUR FAULTY THINKING.

THAT'S ENOUGH!

I'VE COLLECTED A MOUNTAIN OF EVIDENCE IN SUPPORT OF NATURAL SELECTION.

BUT MY CRITICS, AND SEVERAL SUPPORTERS, SEE MY INABILITY TO EXPLAIN HEREDITY AS A GREAT WEAKNESS IN MY THEORY.

SO, WHAT ARE YOU GONNA DO?

NOTHING. I'M OLD AND I'M TIRED.

WHA--? THAT'S NO GOOD. I NEED AN ANSWER!

HELLO?

ARE YOU LISTENING?

PLEASE, SIR. MY MOM IS WATCHING.

I LOST MY MOTHER AS A SMALL CHILD. DO YOU HAVE ANY STORIES ABOUT **THAT?**

NO.

YES.

ONE

WE DON'T TELL IT VERY OFTEN.

120

121

123

124

WHAT'S THE POINT OF TEACHING ME ALL OF THESE STORIES IF YOU WON'T GIVE ME A CHANCE TO TELL THEM TO **MY** CHILDREN?

Sigh.

THIS WILL END BADLY IF YOU DON'T HURRY, SIR.

PLEASE, SIR. I'M STARTING TO LOSE MY GRIP!

BANG YOUR BONES, MARA.

YOU WIN.

ZZ

GOOD NIGHT, ABBA-DUBBA.

ZZz

YES, SO AM I, IT SEEMS.

HAPPY?

YES, SIR. THANK YOU.

ZZz

GOOD LUCK, MARA.

AND, THERE WILL BE NO MORE QUESTIONS, RIGHT?

DON'T WORRY, SIR. YOU WON'T HEAR FROM ME AGAIN.

THE
TRANSMUTATION NOTEBOOK

ANNOTATIONS TO
THE SANDWALK ADVENTURES

The Transmutation Notebook

The idea that species might change over time was originally known as transmutation and had been around long before Charles Darwin made the scene. As you now know, Darwin's contribution to the debate over transmutation (or evolution) was proposing a viable mechanism through which evolution could occur. Darwin developed his theory of Natural Selection after several decades of painstaking observation and experimentation. In the process, he recorded his observations and thoughts about evolution in a series of alphabetically-titled journals he called the Transmutation Notebooks.

These annotations are not required reading to enjoy the story, but they will further explain concepts and provide additional historical information about Darwin's time. I have also provided some background into the research that I did for this book, as well as a bibliography of all sources used.

Endpages

A month or so before my son Max's third birthday, we drew the crayon illustration that appears on the first and last pages of this book. The drawing was actually a surprise to me. One cold Saturday afternoon, Max wanted to draw with crayons at the table. So, there we sat. Max drew purple tornados, while I doodled a quick orange Darwin. After a few minutes, something drew me away (I don't remember what), but I left Max and my orange Darwin on the table. A few minutes later, I heard a small voice from the other room. "I did the mites, Daddy." I wasn't sure what this meant, so I thought I better take a look. What I found floored me. Max had taken my sketch and added two surprisingly recognizable mites at the bottom. I reproduce it here with a healthy dose of fatherly pride.

Chapter 1
God's Follicle

Full Disclosure

Follicle mites don't have eyes. I apologize for this concession to the conventions of cartooning and storytelling. They don't have uvulas, either. Oh, and they don't talk. Just wanted to be clear on that.

Page 11

I used an illustration by Conrad Martens as visual reference for the beached Great Ship. Martens was the replacement artist on the *Beagle*'s voyage, taking the place of the ailing Augustus Earle. Darwin apparently liked Martens quite a bit and shared his enthusiasm for the work they were doing. Martens eventually left the voyage in 1835 to settle in Australia.

The original illustration depicts repair work being done by the *Beagle*'s crew on the beach of some distant shore. The copy I used for reference was from Janet Browne's *Charles Darwin: Voyaging*. The drawing was originally commissioned for *Narrative*, Captain Robert Fitzroy's 1839 travelogue of the *Beagle*'s voyage.

Pages 11-15

I started my last book with a myth and here is another one. Color me formulaic. My wife, Lisa, would prefer that I just skip the myths and get on with the story, but I think they're a great vehicle for understanding the way we try to make sense of the world. That's not to say Lisa doesn't like the myths, she just doesn't like to see me start with them.

Page 1

Darwin was the naturalist on the *HMS Beagle* for most of the ship's five-year voyage (1831-1836). He was originally hired on as a dinner guest for the ship's captain, Robert Fitzroy, but became the full-time naturalist when the ship's surgeon-naturalist, Robert McCormick, quit.

Darwin's voyage on the *Beagle* was the turning point in his life. Much to his father's chagrin, Charles had failed as a physician and jumped at the opportunity to join the *Beagle*'s crew before finishing his work to become a clergyman. Dr. Robert Darwin was convinced that this trip would destroy his son's chance at being well settled. He once told Charles, "You care for nothing but shooting, dogs and rat-catching, and you will be a disgrace to yourself and all your family." This probably wasn't fair (and it certainly wasn't an accurate prediction), but Charles did have a passion for collecting and shooting. He would get the opportunity to do more than his share of both on the *Beagle*.

One of the interesting elements of the voyage was its beginning, or, to be more accurate, its three beginnings. The *Beagle* set sail on Dec 10th, 1831, but it soon returned to port due to bad weather. Eleven days later, on the 21st, the weather was good enough to leave, and so they did. And they promptly ran aground. After getting loose, they sailed out to sea, only to be turned back again the next morning by bad weather. They finally got underway successfully on Dec 27th.

Page 12

Darwin had a couple of nicknames while on the *Beagle*. To his shipmates, he was "the dear old Philosopher," and many of the crew, who liked Darwin quite a bit, called him "our flycatcher."

Page 13

Since it was low tide when the *Beagle* ran aground on Dec 21st, the only way the crew could free the ship was to rock it loose by running back and forth along the deck.

Pages 13-14

Darwin never seemed to grow very sturdy sea legs and spent much of his 5 years on the *Beagle* being seasick.

Page 14, last panel

Darwin's iconic white beard did not actually appear until several decades after his trip on the *Beagle*. In fact, when he wrote the *Origin of the Species* he didn't have a beard and his hair wasn't yet gray.

The beardless Charles Darwin

Page 15

Darwin collected crates and crates of plant, animal and fossil specimens from all over the world. Most were sent back to England, where they were analyzed by experts. The result was that Darwin's work as a naturalist and collector of species helped him make a name for himself in English academic circles even before his return in 1836.

Of course, there was another famous individual in a creation story that named the animals. Genesis 2: 19-20: *19 Out of the ground the LORD God formed every beast of the field and every bird of the air, and brought them to Adam to see what he would call them. And whatever Adam called each living creature, that was its name. 20 So Adam gave names to all cattle, to the birds of the air, and to every beast of the field. But for Adam there was not found a helper comparable to him.* (NKJV)

Did I mention that follicle mites don't have eyes? Just checking.

Page 17

At the end of his life, Darwin focused his energies on worms. They fascinated him and despite feeling very tired and old, Darwin published *The Formation of Vegetable Mould, through the Action of Worms, with Observations on their Habits* o n October 1881. Six months later, on April 19, 1882, he died at home.

Page 20

Emma Darwin was the daughter of Elizabeth and Josiah Wedgwood II and granddaughter of Josiah Wedgwood I, the founder of Wedgwood china. She married Charles in 1839, three years after his return to England. By all accounts, they were deeply in love for the entirety of their 43 years of marriage.

Their relationship is interesting because it is a microcosm for many of the cultural events swirling around the theory of Natural Selection. Emma was a devout Unitarian and was openly troubled by Charles' theories. She wrote her husband two letters, one right after their marriage and the second in 1861, expressing her fears for his soul and the path in which his work was taking him. Darwin would refer to the first of these as Emma's "beautiful letter."

Emma Darwin

The anxiety his work caused his wife pained Darwin, but the evidence supporting his theory was more than he could ignore. Nevertheless, Emma was always there for Charles, and he got nervous when they were separated. She was his constant companion and caregiver in his numerous cycles of illness

Page 22, panel 2

Darwin rested a lot. This was because his work exhausted him and he was often sick. The question of Charles' perpetually bad health has been the subject of some debate. Was he the victim of congenital sickliness or was his ill health the result of the stress and strain of his work? Perhaps Darwin suffered from Chagas disease contracted on his *Beagle* voyage? Did his fear of the notoriety and controversy he knew his theory would generate in Victorian society make him a nervous wreck?

Darwin's mother was a sickly woman and died when Charles was just a boy. Darwin himself had ten children, three of whom died young. Several of the remaining seven were sickly themselves. So, it seems reasonable to assume that Charles was predisposed to being sickly. Was it Chagas disease? No one knows. But we can be fairly confident that his work was very stressful for him and would have only exacerbated his sickly tendencies.

Page 24, last panel

Darwin's home was called Down House and was located in the village of Downe, Kent. The fireplace depicted here is the one in Darwin's new study (as are the bookshelves and window on page 10). The new study was completed late in Darwin's life, and it was here that he finished his book on earthworms. The study depicted in this story is currently the gift shop in Down House. The study on display at Down House is the old study where Darwin wrote *The Origin of Species*. So, when you see a picture of his study, you are probably seeing the old study, with its simpler fireplace and the big mirror on the mantle. Now you know.

Page 26, panel 1

Routine figured fairly prominently in Darwin's daily life. Dinner was at 7:30 every night and was followed by two games of backgammon with Emma. Then Charles would read and listen to Emma play the piano. This is important to keep in mind when considering Emma's comment on page 16 when Darwin says he's going to the sandwalk. He didn't usually go to the sandwalk until noon, and it was only 11 am. Would this deviation from schedule surprise Emma? I don't know. But I had her comment on it just the same. His daily schedule is listed below:

7:45 – Breakfast alone
8:00 – 9:30 Work in study
9:30 – 10:30 Read letters or listen as Emma read to him
10:30 – 12:00 More work in study
12:00 – Walk on the sandwalk
1:00 – 3:00 Lunch, read the newspaper and reply to letters
3:00 – 4:00 Rest in his bedroom; sometimes, Emma would read to him
4:00 - 4:30 A short walk
4:30 - 5:30 More work in the study
7:30 – Dinner, backgammon and piano
8:30 – Bed
(from *Down: The Home of the Darwins*, by Sir Hedley Atkins, KBE).

Panels 1-4

A number of historians point to Charles' apparent fear of losing his mind. Although he seemed to be resigned to his body betraying him, he desperately feared losing his mental faculties. I was inspired to play on this portion of Darwin's psyche by my friend and fellow cartoonist John Kerschbaum.

For the first issue of this comic series, I asked John to draw me his rendition of Darwin, which I would then place on my back cover. When I got the package from John, I was delighted to find two Darwin drawings (shown below). The first was the serious fellow we all know and love. John, however, wasn't happy with the dour Darwin and produced a slightly more unhinged version that more closely reflected his sensibilities as a cartoonist.

The Kerschbaum Darwins

Now, up to this point, it had not been my intention for there to be any direct interaction between Mara and Darwin. I had planned to have Mara and Willy observe Darwin and those in his life and work the ideas out for themselves. Yawn. Fortunately for me (and the story), John's second image inspired me to explore a conversation between Darwin and Mara that would have Darwin constantly questioning his sanity. Thanks, John.

Polly was Emma and Charles' daughter Henrietta's white fox terrier and was a regular companion for Charles on the sandwalk.

Of course, the walking stick is wrong. I have an explanation, honest. It all started when I was waiting for a meeting to start in Juniata's Beeghly library. I was browsing their books on Darwin, and as I flipped through Huxley and Kettlewell's *Darwin and His World*, I came across a picture of Darwin's walking stick on page 119. "Ooo," I thought, "this is so cool! What a find." Then I looked at my watch and realized that the meeting was starting in a minute, and I didn't

want to walk in late on the Provost. So, I absent-mindedly put the book back on the shelf and ran.

A few months later, as I was drawing the first chapter of this book, I went looking for the walking stick picture. I thought it was in one of the books I had in my possession, and I proceeded to go crazy looking for it. Gah! And of course, by this time, I had forgotten my visit in the library, and I needed to draw the scenes with his walking stick. So, I made it rough-hewn, because I was sure it had some shape to it, and forged ahead.

Then, a year later, as I was completing the final pages of the fifth and final chapter, I had another meeting in the library. I found myself browsing the Darwin books for a picture of his family crest and, as I did – BOOM! – there it was again, taunting me: a photo of the walking stick leaning against a wicker chair sitting on the verandah of Down House. A groove made by a climbing plant spirals up the walking stick to give it a unique shape.

The walking stick accurately drawn
(well, except that it isn't to scale, of course)

Page 27, the sandwalk

The sandwalk was an invaluable refuge for Darwin and his thoughts. No matter the weather, Darwin would walk the path at noon everyday. The sandwalk itself was across the home meadow from Down House on the Darwin estate. Although he used it the entire time he was at Down House,

Darwin actually rented the sandwalk for 32 years (first from John Lubbock I and later from his son John II).

In 1874, Darwin bought it from the younger Lubbock, who asked a pretty penny for the little strip of land. Their friendship suffered for it. I have included a map of the grounds of Down House below. It is taken from Figure 10 in *The Darwin Legend* by James Moore and originally appeared in Hedley Atkin's book *Down, the Home of the Darwins*.

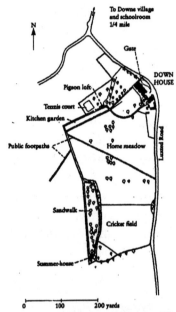

Darwin's estate and Down House

Page 27, water therapy

In the early 1840s, Darwin desperately sought relief from the mysterious illness afflicting him. Dr. James Gully's Water Cure Establishment in Malvern came highly recommended by a number of people close to him. Darwin was suspicious of the notion and read Gully's book. The therapy apparently involved dousing the patient in cold water to improve the circulation and draw the blood supply away from the inflamed nerves of the stomach. Despite his

initial reservations, Darwin became a true believer and depended on the therapy. He was desperate several years later when a scandal threatened Dr. Gully's practice.

Page 29, panel 1

In the summer of 1855, Charles' attention turned to pigeons. He became a regular companion of breeders and pigeon fanciers as he bred pigeons, selecting for small variations each generation, and created numerous varieties. This *artificial* selection was a fundamental piece of supporting evidence for *natural* selection. In fact, *Variation Under Domestication* is the first chapter of *Origin of the Species*. Pigeons figure prominently in the subsection *Breeds of the Domestic Pigeon, their Differences and Origins*.

Page 30, last panel

Here Mara asks the crucial question: **How?** This is the question that scientists ask. Darwin couldn't answer her earlier question, "**Why** do we exist?" because that's a metaphysical question and consequently sits outside the realm of science - just as the **How** of our existence sits outside the realm of metaphysics.

Chapter 2
The Stone Path

Page 36

Mara's stuttering here is based on something I picked up a long time ago about Moses. Somewhere along the way in my life as a student, I heard that Moses stuttered. During the preparation of this chapter, I started to wonder how historians or theologians could know this. A quick sweep of an online Bible concordance yielded only one scripture that seems relevant, namely Exodus 4:10: *And Moses said unto the LORD, O my Lord, I am not eloquent, neither heretofore, nor since thou hast spoken unto thy servant: but I am slow of speech, and of a slow tongue.* (KJV)

Page 40

In 1995, my wife and I went to Cambridge, England, for a Neuroethology meeting. This was long before I had imagined doing a Darwin book, so I didn't visit Darwin's home or stroll along his sandwalk. Consequently, I have neither visual reference material nor the context of experience from which to draw the sandwalk scenes.

Things looked bleak for my attempts at visual authenticity until I found a terrific web page called *AboutDarwin.com*. Among a wide array of fun Darwin stuff, this site has a photo stroll around the sandwalk.

Page 41

The age of the world was very much a subject of debate in Darwin's time. Estimates were made based on things ranging from the number of generations in the Bible to the temperature of the earth. In the late 1860's, Charles got a bit concerned when Lord Kelvin's cooling earth theory placed the earth's age at 20 million years. If this had been true, it would make the Earth far too young for gradual evolutionary change to explain life's enormous diversity. Fortunately for Darwin, Kelvin's estimates were skewed by the presence of radioactive isotopes in the earth. Current calculations of the earth's age by geologists using radioisotope decay indicate that the Earth is about 4.5 billion years old. That is plenty of time for Charlie's pet project.

Page 42

As young boys, Darwin and his brother, Erasmus, built a chemistry laboratory in the back garden of The Mount, their family estate. A converted old washroom served as a lab that housed all of the chemicals and equipment the two boys could scrape together.

When Erasmus left for Cambridge University in 1822, Darwin assumed control of the lab and continued his work on crystallography and the chemical analyses of minerals. His experiments, however, were not confined to the lab. As a boarding student at the nearby Shrewsbury School, he acquired the nickname "Gas" because of his late-night, bedside chemistry experiments with a blowpipe and an open flame.

When you consider that the odors from his experiments mixed with the stench of a 30-boy attic dormitory, it's a wonder Charles wasn't tossed out by his classmates.

Panels 4 - 5

According to most biographers, Darwin was no whiz with figures. While at Cambridge University, he struggled with basic algebra and arithmetic. His 3-day final exams culminated in a daylong mathematics test. Darwin passed, but not with much room to spare.

The inability to multiply 6 x 14 in my story is a fictional invention for comic relief. I hope that it humanizes the iconic Darwin. It is not my intent to detract from his genius.

During Darwin's one year of medical school at Edinburgh University, geology was all the rage. Charles was one of hundreds of people who attended courses taught by the University's two rival geologists, Hope and Jameson. It was in these lecture halls that his interest in geology was first kindled.

Later, as a student at Cambridge, Darwin was introduced by his mentor John Henslow to the Reverend Adam Sedgwick. Sedgwick was a professor of geology at Cambridge and was looking for a companion for a geology expedition he was taking to North Wales. The trip was an invaluable educational experience. Darwin quickly learned to identify mineral and fossil specimens and interpret strata.

Charles Lyell

Charles Lyell's impact on Darwin was equally significant. Lyell revived and expanded upon the work of a Scottish geologist named James Hutton. Both Hutton and Lyell believed that the Earth was a dynamic sphere, shaped by natural forces such as wind, rain, erosion and volcanic activity.

While Hutton published this theory of uniform change in 1788, it wasn't until Lyell developed it and popularized it in his book *Principles of Geology* in 1830 that it replaced the notion of a static, unchanging Earth. Before this, the prevailing Catastrophic Theory attempted to explain the geological record as a series of global catastrophes (Noah's flood being the most recent) that cleansed the Earth of all life. According to this theory, the world was made, destroyed and remade multiple times, and each stratum in the earth's crust contained the fossil remains of the species that lived between catastrophes. Lyell's answer was simpler.

While Lyell became a friend of Darwin, he never fully accepted the concept of the organic evolution of species. His doubts were exacerbated by the death of his wife, after which he became deeply concerned with the existence of a soul. Nevertheless, his ideas were essential for paving the way for Darwin's Theory of Natural Selection

Thomas Henry Huxley (nicknamed Darwin's Bulldog for his ferocious defense of Darwin's ideas) said of Lyell, "I cannot but believe that Lyell was for others, as for me, the chief agent for smoothing the road for Darwin." I would love to tell you that Huxley's words inspired the Smooth Stone Path of Understanding, but the truth is that I didn't come across this quote until I was preparing these annotations.

It is important to note, however, that despite his staunch support of Darwin, Huxley was never behind the process of natural selection 100%. Huxley heralded Darwin's *Origin of the Species* as the start of a new epoch in science, and he became an ardent advocate for evolution. But he felt Darwin's Theory of Natural Selection relied too heavily on gradualism. Nevertheless, he was Darwin's most aggressive lieutenant and played a significant role in selling evolution to the layperson.

Thomas Henry Huxley

Panel 7

A colleague in the Geology Department pointed out to me that the Earth's crust is much thinner than I have illustrated here. In actuality, if the Earth was an apple, the crust would only be as thick as the apple peel.

Page 46

Despite the fact that Darwin read Lyell's *Principles* on the voyage of the *Beagle*, there is no indication that Darwin was thinking about evolution at the time. However, Lyell's ideas about the age of the Earth created a revolutionary contextual shift for Darwin. Years later, when he was working on his Theory of Natural Selection, the concept of small, gradual changes in species over long periods of time was central to his thinking.

Page 47

The voyage of the *Beagle* was a mapping mission of the South American coast. Captain Fitzroy was the cartographer, an aristocratic Tory and the reason Darwin was on the *Beagle* in the first place. Seems Fitzroy needed someone from his own social station to dine with during the voyage. Henslow recommended Darwin for the position, knowing how eager he would be to see the fauna and geology of the world

Robert Fitzroy

Fitzroy always comes off as a proud, stuffed shirt in most of the things I've read, so he gets to be a peacock in my book. Even worse, his dabbling in pseudoscience almost cost Darwin the job. Fitzroy was a physiognomist and believed that a person's character could be judged by the proportions of his or her features. During their first meeting, Fitzroy became concerned that Darwin's big nose suggested laziness. Fortunately, he overcame his rhinophobic tendencies and took Darwin on. Anything but lazy, Darwin went on to become one of the most prodigious collectors in the history of natural science. Of course, in this, he had a head start.

Darwin had been honing his collecting skills since he was a young boy. He drove his father and the rest of his family to distraction with his voluminous collections of everything from bird eggs to beetles. However, what had appeared at the time to be a trivial pursuit was, in fact, building the skills he would need to begin the work that would one day fundamentally change the way we view nature.

Page 48

Darwin enjoyed his time with the gauchos. Despite the general bad health he suffered later in life, Darwin appears to have been more rough-and-tumble as a young man (on land, at least). He never did see that jaguar, though.

I used the beautiful plates from Alan Morehead's *Darwin and the Beagle* as reference for the gauchos' attire. I couldn't find the name of the artist credited for the paintings.

Page 49

Mr. Keane (or Keen, depending on the source) is a bit of a mystery, but he is presumed to have been an Englishman by those historians that even mention him.

The Sarandis is a small stream entering Uruguay's Rio Negro.

Visual reference for the *Toxodon* skull was taken from figures in *The Zoology of the Voyage of HMS Beagle*.

The giant sloth is a composite of images from all of the dinosaur/prehistoric life books I've collected since I was a kid.

Page 51

Darwin made several fossil discoveries that had a tremendous impact on the scientific community at the time. Of course, the most significant impact the fossils had were on Darwin himself. Here, Darwin saw worlds of life that were long gone. Critical to the theory he would formulate years later was his observation that many of the fossil organisms had striking similarities to organisms alive in the 1800s. Giant sloths looked like the tree sloths of his time. The armored *Glypdodont* looked like a giant armadillo. Details and size had changed over time, but the basic body plans were unchanged, in most cases. Within the context of Lyell's dynamically changing Earth, Darwin could see with certainty that life wasn't destroyed every millennium, as the Catastrophic Theory held. Life was changing gradually in response to a dynamically changing environment.

Page 51

Sir Richard Owen was the preeminent comparative anatomist of Darwin's time and analyzed the mammalian fossils that Darwin collected while on the *Beagle*. He also coined the term "dinosaur" and first came to my attention when I was a dinosaur enthusiast as a small boy. Owen collaborated with sculptor Benjamin Waterhouse Hawkins to construct life-sized models of the dinosaurs *Iguanodon*, *Megalosaurus* and *Hylaeosaurus* for the grounds of London's Crystal Palace. To celebrate the upcoming debut of the dinosaur models, Owen and Hawkins held a dinner for 20 esteemed guests in the belly of the unfinished *Iguanodon*. This sounded so cool to me at the time that I still have a vivid memory of the artist's rendering of the dinner in the dinosaur. I've seen it reproduced in a number of dinosaur books. After a quick scan of those on my bookshelf, I found it on page 9 of the *Dinosaur* book in the Eyewitness Books series.

Richard Owen

Owen is also credited with identifying a type of organism important for *The Sandwalk Adventures*. In the 1840s Owen described follicle mites and named their genus *Demodex* ("lard worm.") They aren't worms, of course, but members of the Subclass *Arachnida*. This subclass includes spiders, scorpions, ticks and mites. Armed with this information, you can now join those of us who take great pleasure in pointing out to people at parties that spiders aren't insects.

Anyway, back to Owen. Despite their initial collaboration, Darwin and Owen eventually became bitter enemies when Owen began opposing Darwin and his Theory of Natural Selection. In a way, it seems appropriate that the little pest bothering Darwin throughout this story was discovered by a big pest that bothered Darwin during most of his professional life.

According to Desmond and Moore, Darwin really did ride back to Montevideo with the skull on his lap. What a nut.

Page 53

The extinct animals in Darwin's field include an *Iguanodon* in the foreground, a *Smilodon* (sabre-toothed tiger) on the left, an elephant-like creature called *Ambelodon* on the right, an *Apatosaurus* in back and a generic pterosaur in the air. One of our relatives is peeking over the hedge.

The first statement in the lower panel paraphrases something Darwin wrote while in the midst of a fossil-hunting frenzy: *"The pleasure of the first day's partridge shooting...cannot be compared to finding a fine group of fossil bones, which tell their story of former times with almost a living tongue."*

Page 55

It is important to note that, as convincing as the fossil record is that life HAS changed, it doesn't address HOW life has changed. This is an important consideration because many non-evolutionists accepted the existence of fossils; they just created other explanations for the absence of these creatures today (*e.g.* the Catastrophic Theory).

Chapter 3
Darwin Saves the World

Page 59

This was a very hard page to draw. I got it into my head that the opening shot of Down House had to be from the air. I tried to talk myself out of it, but to no avail. When I went looking for pictures of the home, I was *shocked* to discover no aerial shots existed of Darwin's home. Fortunately, there have been plenty of photos taken of the house at ground level. Using these photos, I tried to get a feel for the shape of the house and then rotate it in my mind. This wouldn't have been such an ordeal if Mr. Darwin's home were a nice, neat box, but it isn't. It started that way, though. When it was built as a farmhouse in 1650, it was fairly simple. An addition in 1778 maintained the nice, neat boxiness. However, in 1842, when the Darwins moved in, that all started to change.

The Darwins were living in London in 1842. Darwin had been developing his Theory of Natural Selection and was petrified of the social implications publishing would bring. He had witnessed the public hounding and humiliation of evolutionists by the Church and Tory establishment, and the threatening tenor of the debate made him anxious to get out of town. On July 22, he and Emma visited the village of Downe to examine what would one day be their home. Charles described the house as "square and unpretending." In 1843, a year after moving in, they had the first addition added to the house. Three more followed in 1858, 1872 and 1877. The result was something confoundingly difficult for me draw. Of course, my struggle was exacerbated by an on-going battle with perspective. I worked on it for four morning before work. The end result is my best approximation of the house from above.

I want to thank David Leff of *AboutDarwin.com* for providing a vast collection of online reference photos of Down House. He also told me that Darwin's bedroom window was the big bay window on the second floor at the back of the house.

Page 60, Panel 1

Desmond and Moore point out in their excellent biography of Darwin that illness was a way of life at Down House. Emma was the head of the hospital and was known for her kind ministrations to her family, as well as to the people of the village of Downe. Emma had spent a good portion of her life caring for her sickly sister, mother, husband and children. She was also almost perpetually pregnant into her forties. She understood pain and discomfort and had the empathy to soothe both.

Sir Francis Darwin was the seventh of ten children born to Emma and Charles. He became his father's scientific partner and moved in with his parents after his wife, Amy Ruck, died of a convulsive fever four days after giving birth to Darwin's grandson Bernard. After Charles' death, Francis became a Professor of Botany at Cambridge University from 1884-1904 and was knighted in 1913.

Panel 2

The Darwins had two butlers during Charles Darwin's life. Joseph Parslow was the first and joined the Darwin household in 1839 while they were still living in London. He was with the family for 36 years until he retired in 1875. Parslow was succeeded by a former groom named William Jackson. Jackson was described lovingly by Bernard as a jolly, funny man. This story takes place late in Darwin's life when Jackson was the butler.

Page 62

I learned of the stone-kicking ritual from a video designed to solicit funds for the renovation of Down House. The narrator of the video was the great English naturalist Sir David Attenborough. He even gave a little demonstration. The video was a file included on the CD-ROM *The complete works of Charles Darwin* (2001), by Lightbinders.

Page 63

Here we begin a discussion of Darwin's major contribution to evolutionary thought. The four postulates that I present here were not specifically enumerated in *Origin of the Species*. However, most texts break the following passage from the Introduction to *Origin* into four parts.

"As many more individuals of each species are born than can possibly survive; and as, consequently, there is a frequently recurring struggle for existence, it follows that any being, if it vary however slightly in any manner profitable to itself, under the complex and sometimes varying conditions of life, will have a better chance of surviving, and thus be naturally selected. From the strong principle of inheritance, any selected variety will tend to propagate its new and modified form."

One of the complaints often made by opponents of Darwin's Theory of Natural Selection is that it is not falsifiable, and thus not scientific. Some go so far as to suggest that it is ultimately based on faith. This is an erroneous argument. Each of the four postulates outlined in the passage above can be tested and, potentially, proven false. That means natural selection meets the criteria for being considered scientific. Let's take them individually in the order they were presented in the story.

1. Individuals within a species are variable.

Just looking at the people around you is enough to demonstrate that humans are variable. The same can be said of almost every other type of living thing in the world (there are some organisms that reproduce clonally). These differences, and their potential worth, are inherently acknowledged in our own language with phrases and terms like "pick of the litter" and "runt."

2. Some of an individual's variations are passed onto its offspring.

Most children resemble their parents. Some people say my son Max looks like me. Others say that he has Lisa's chin. Max resembles Lisa and me because he has inherited a specific set of genes from us. Of course, Darwin never knew about genes and DNA, but his observations about the obvious process of inheritance and its implications for his Theory of Natural Selection are still valid.

You may have noticed I began this particular postulate with the qualifying word "some." Not all variations are passed on to offspring. If an organism *acquires* a trait during its lifetime, the trait is not passed on to its offspring. Say, for example, a lizard loses its tail to a predator, but the lizard survives and reproduces. The lizard's offspring won't be tailless, because the lizard will still carry, and consequently pass on, the genes required to make a tail

3. More offspring are produced than survive.

Let's consider the ocean sunfish (*Mola mola*) as an extreme example.

A single female may produce as many as 300 million eggs. Such a reproductive feat has earned *Mola mola* bragging rights as the most fecund vertebrate. Now, if one *Mola mola* is capable of producing that many eggs, why aren't the oceans choked with an overabundance of sunfish? The reason is that most of the eggs and the subsequent juvenile fish are consumed by predators or don't survive for some other reason. Few live long enough to reproduce.

4. Those offspring that survive and reproduce have inherited a variation that gives them an advantage.

It doesn't require seeing many National Geographic specials to know that predators like lions target young and weak members of a herd. The healthier and stronger or faster you are, the more likely you are to a) avoid being targeted by a predator or b) survive an attack. If the advantage that helps an organism survive is something controlled by its genes, then if it survives and reproduces, it may pass those genes (and consequently, the advantage) on to its offspring.

It should be fairly clear in the descriptions I have given above that genes are pretty important when considering how natural selection works. The incorporation of genetics into Darwin's Theory of Natural Selection has led to what is known as the Modern Synthesis. In the Modern Synthesis, the four postulates are updated a touch. I present them here as they appear in *Evolutionary Analysis* (2nd ed.) by Freemon and Herron, 2001. You will notice that they use the term 'allele' in these postulates instead of 'gene', so a little explanation is in order.

We are all born with two gene copies for almost every trait. We get one from our mother and one from our father. Most traits are controlled by several genes, but there are a number of single-gene traits. The ability to roll your tongue is controlled by one gene. In that gene we see two different variations, or **alleles**. One allele gives you the ability to roll your tongue (the

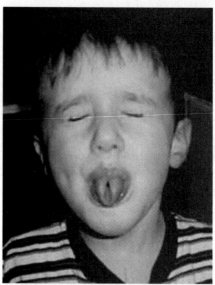

"Don't stick your tongue out at me, young man!"
Tongue rolling: a single gene trait.

dominant allele) and the other does not (the recessive allele). There are 3 possible combinations of these 2 alleles. If you have two recessive alleles, you won't be able to roll your tongue. Folks with one or two of the dominant alleles are tongue rollers. My wife and I can both roll our tongues, and so can our eldest son, Max. The jury is still out on 7-month-old Jack. I have included a picture above of Max displaying his tongue rolling proficiency. It took 51 attempts with the digital camera to get this picture. I tried 42 before I gave up and handed the camera over to Lisa.

As the expert picture taker in our family, she got this shot in 9 tries.

OK, so let's get back to the updated postulates of Natural Selection (finally). They are:

1. As a result of mutation creating new alleles, and segregation and independent assortment shuffling alleles into new combinations, individuals within a population are variable for nearly all traits.

2. Individuals pass their alleles on to their offspring intact.

3. In most generations, more offspring are produced than can survive.

4. The individuals that survive and go on to reproduce, or who reproduce the most, are those with alleles and allele combinations that best adapt them to their environment.

Page67

Annie was the second child born to the Darwins and Charles' favorite. She died of tuberculosis at the age of ten, and Darwin was crushed by the loss. He wept over her photograph for the rest of his life, and his faith in God was irrevocably shattered by the experience.

Page 68

Mites don't have an anus because they really don't "need" one. They feed upon the fluid (called cytoplasm) in your hair-follicle cells, and their mouthparts form a fine filter that prevents them from taking in the very small cellular organelles. As a result, mites live on a fluid diet consisting of material that, because it is in the cell, has already been digested. This makes their digestive system so efficient that they don't produce much waste

Page 70

My graduate advisor, Harald Esch, explained fitness to his Animal Behavior class at Notre Dame in the following way. He pointed out that a priest who was a world-class Olympian, terrifically strong and fast, would have a Darwinian fitness of zero because he had no children. It was pretty effective, given the context. I always opted for the example of a fight between the Hulk and Superman. No matter who the winner, it is not the survival of the fittest, because (as far as I know) neither has children.

The term *survival of the fittest* did not appear in the first edition of *Origin of the Species*. The term was coined by a contemporary of Darwin named Herbert Spencer in his book *Principles in Biology*. Darwin didn't think Spencer's book really said all that much, and he found it tedious to get through. However, at the time Darwin was under a lot of fire for the anthropomorphic nature of the term *natural selection* and was looking for a term that would transcend that criticism. He incorporated survival of the fittest in the sixth and final edition of *Origin*.

Page 73

Why beetles? Darwin was a beetle-collecting fiend during his college days at Cambridge. In fact, beetle collecting was all the rage with the Victorian set at the time.

Why *purple* beetles? I started coloring the cover to this issue before I had started drawing this page. I was looking for a color for the beetles, and Lisa pointed out that I rarely use purple. I have since rectified that situation.

The sequence with Kor-Guu is taken from one of the one-page science cartoons I used to draw for The Ohio State University Entomology Department newsletter. There was no Polly the Wonder Dog and Darwin wasn't nearly so vigorous, but the joke was basically the same.

Chapter 4
The Application of Pressure

Page 83

Stories, like the languages that convey them, have the ability to change over time. An oral tradition is perpetuated by passing stories and myths on to the next generation. But most of us know how unreliable people can be when it comes to telling a story exactly as it was told to them. Most storytellers like to add a little of themselves to a tale. These little changes might be viewed as "mutations" in the story. If they are received well by the audience, then they will be passed along to others, but if they aren't popular, they are likely to disappear altogether. Thus, stories can change over time to suit their environment (in this case, the audience). When more than one successful variation of a story survives, we find differences in a single story that may have specific regional or historical distinctions. In this case, in the environment defined by Mara's audience, more sensationalistic stories seem to be more adaptive.

Page 85, panel 3

Mara's brother Campbell is named for Joseph Campbell, whose book *The Hero with a Thousand Faces* examines the unifying elements of the hero's story (or, in our case, heroine's story) in most of the world's mythologies.

Page 88

Considering where this story takes place and my proclivity for things like butt jokes, the appearance of a giant zit should come as no surprise to anyone. In this story, the zit represents a potential **selective pressure**. A selective pressure is something that does the selecting in natural selection. For example, predation is a selective pressure on a population of prey, favoring those individuals that have the adaptations to avoid being eaten over those that lack them (or have them to a lesser degree).

The relationship between follicle mites and acne is an interesting one. There is anecdotal evidence that some types of acne around the eyes and nose may be the result of an allergy to follicle mites. While Darwin had many maladies, I have seen no indication that acne was one of them.

Page 89

In his article "Body Beasts," in the December 1998 *National Geographic Magazine*, Richard Coniff notes that the rich flora that once inhabited our skin has been reduced to primarily bacteria and follicle mites. Oh, sure -- fleas and ticks stop by occasionally for blood meals, and every once in awhile lice find their way back, but bacteria and follicle mites are the only ones that we haven't been able to shake.

While there is no scientific evidence to support the notion that bacteria sing, they do take their reproduction seriously. The primary approach they use is by dividing asexually (a process known as fission). However, they do get sexy every once in awhile. Sometimes, one bacterium forms a straw-like connection (called a conjugation tube) with another bacterium. Through this tube, the two bacteria can exchange bits and pieces of genetic material. This exchange helps to add variety to each of the bacterium's genetic make-up, and, as we know, variety is the spice of life (and the fodder for evolution)

Pages 92 - 93

The exchange between Darwin and a desperate Mara was actually inspired by Robert Pennock's book *Tower of Babel: The Evidence against the New Creationism*. This book offers a lucid explanation of the many factions of the creationist movement. In panel 5 of page 10, Mara is a Young Earth Creationist (YEC). YECs hold to the literal translation of the Genesis story and believe that the earth is no more than 6000 years old.

After the cosmic dope slap at the top of page 11, Mara adopts the views of the Mature Earth Creationists (MEC). MECs believe that the earth is 6000 years old, but that God just made it LOOK like it was 4.5 billion years old. (I've always thought this view made God look as much like a deceiver as a creator.)

Another whack to the head and in the last panel of page 11, Mara is suddenly proposing ideas supported by Progressive Evolutionists (PE), who believe that life and the universe have evolved in accordance with natural laws with God stepping in, as Pennock puts it, "at strategic points along the way."

Tower of Babel is an excellent book for anyone who wants a primer in the basic points of evolutionary theory, a history of creationist thought and an examination the current state of the evolution/creationism debate.

Page 95

This page is dedicated to my wife, Lisa, for all of the support she has given me in the production of this book.

The specific décor of Darwin's bedroom is invariably incorrect because I just made it up. (Wouldn't it be amazing if I guessed correctly, though...?) I did, however, strive for authenticity. To this end, the excellent PBS series *Evolution* came in handy. The first episode ("Darwin's Dangerous Idea") alternates between a discussion of current evolutionary problems and a period costume drama of Darwin working out his theory. In one scene of the drama, Darwin and his brother, Erasmus, are discussing the merits of marriage as Darwin dresses himself. The candles, vase, chair, wall hangings, dressing mirror and small tables are taken from the video. The bed is totally wrong, but I failed to consider its authenticity when I drew it in the third chapter. Thus, I drew myself into a corner and was faced with the question of accuracy or consistency. I chose the latter.

Page 96

Here we begin a discussion of one of the most misunderstood elements of evolution: Individuals don't evolve. I dread the day the Pokemon generation starts going to college, because there will be a lot of unlearning that needs to be done.

Of course, "evolving" someone is a staple of science fiction. Invariably when someone is evolved (or "de-evolved" as in *Dr. Jekyll and Mr. Hyde* or the movie *Altered States*), it is by some tricky use of radiation, drugs, genetic engineering, or whatever science is fashionable at the time. "Evolved" individuals usually have gigantic craniums or greatly enhanced minds that give them telepathy or telekinesis, or they become beings of pure energy. These transformations often occur because the "treatment" has unlocked the genetic or evolutionary "potential" being bottled up by our own inadequacies as humans -- social commentary and science misfact in one big mélange. In the end, it incorrectly suggests that these transformations are inevitabilities. But, as I hope you know by now, there are no inevitabilities in evolution.

Page 97

Jellyfish and squid both use jet propulsion. In each case, they use muscular contractions to draw water into a part of their body and then force it out through a smaller hole. This generates a propulsive force that pushes the animals around. Squid are particularly good at it and can move up to 23 miles/hour. In some cases, they actually move fast enough to shoot out of the water.

Panel 6

The "no butt" thing was supposed to be a throwaway joke in the first chapter of this story. I never dreamed I could get this much mileage out of it, but it keeps coming back as a good example of the topic at hand. My apologies if you are not a fan of scatological humor.

Page 99, panel 2

The "March of Progress" is probably one of the most recognizable pictorial depictions of evolution. It is also very misleading. There is no "progress" in evolution as we tend to envision it. Aristotle saw life as a ladder of forms with humans at the top and animals on the rungs below getting less and less complex as you descend the ladder. This notions suggests, for example, that all amphibians are just waiting around to evolve into reptiles or that bacteria are sitting down at the bottom of the ladder hankering to get off the bench and evolve into something more interesting.

But evolution isn't necessarily a process of increasing complexity. It is a process of surviving the prevailing environmental conditions. In that context (and any other context, for that matter), bacteria are the most successful living things on the planet. They live miles below the earth, high into the mountains, in the sea, in the hot springs of Yellowstone, in the air, all over you (despite you best attempts in the shower) and even in the acidic

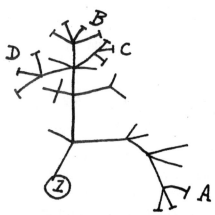

An early evolutionary tree from Darwin's notebooks (redrawn from a page reproduced in __Charles Darwin: Voyaging__, by Janet Browne)

realm of your stomach! The fact that they have existed as they do for the entire history of life is a testament to how evolutionarily successful their simple design has been.

Among Darwin's significant contributions to evolutionary thought was to visualize the evolution of life as a tree (pictured above), instead of a linear progression.

Page 99, panel 5

Single-celled bacteria may be the most successful living things on the planet, but the most successful multicellular animals on Earth are insects. Insects comprise 75% of all known animals species, and the majority of those species are beetles.

The evolutionary success of insects can be attributed to a number of adaptations that have helped them survive in harsh terrestrial environments. Their tough, wax-coated exoskeleton resists desiccation and allowed them to carry a little bit of the ocean with them. But it was wings that really helped insects to take off. The ability to fly allowed insects to disperse great distances and exploit niches before their competitors arrived.

The woodland butterfly drawn here is a Speckled Wood (*Pararge aegeria)* and is a native British species. Individuals don't live for more than a week to ten days, but they are constantly reproducing while the weather is nice

Page 100

No one did more to outline the problems with the Theory of Natural Selection than Darwin himself. He also did quite a bit to try to explain how those difficulties could be solved within his theory. One problem championed by the British comparative anatomist St. George Jackson Mivart was how natural selection could work gradually on an incipient feature to make a structure as complex as a wing.

According to biographers Desmond and Moore, Darwin found Mivart's criticisms "devastating." They were not, however, inexplicable. In the sixth edition of *Origin of the Species*, Darwin added a new chapter ("Miscellaneous Objections") to address many of Mivart's concerns, but it wasn't necessary to add anything to address the concern about gradual wing formation. In the sixth chapter, "Difficulties of the Theory", subsection "Modes of Transition," Darwin outlines his concept of *functional shift*. He even relates some of the latest work on insect wing evolution: "...Landois has shown that the wings of insects are developed from the tracheae; therefore it is highly probable that in this great class organs which once served for respiration have been actually converted into organs for flight." Tracheae are an insect's breathing tubes, so the notion of insect wings coming from the breathing apparatus dates to Darwin's time.

Some very interesting studies have been done to test this hypothesis of functional shift. Kinsolver and Koehl (1985) theorized that wings might have initially developed as heat-collecting devices. They used models to show that as the wings got bigger, they collected more heat and that at a critical point they might reach a length at which they would be useful for flight.

More recent work has been done in the lab of James Marden at The Pennsylvania State University. Marden and his colleagues have proposed that plecopterans (or stoneflies) may offer insight into the

Clioperla clio nymph, external gills

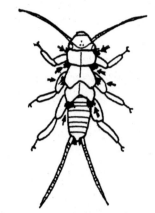

marked with arrows (redrawn from Frison)

origin of insect flight. They suggest that the use of large external gills by stoneflies to skip across the surface of the water could represent a means of locomotion that may have led to more sophisticated flight (and the development of wings) millions of years ago. This would have obvious evolutionary advantages, not the least of which would be to leave the water briefly to confuse a pursuing predator. The juvenile stages of stoneflies are called nymphs, and they are primarily aquatic. I have reproduced a line drawing of a *Clioperla clio* nymph and labeled the prominent external gills.

These days, *functional shift* is often referred to as "preadaptation." In 1982, Elisabeth Vrba and the late Stephen Jay Gould proposed that this term was misleading and proposed that it be changed to "exaptation." I have seen both in my reading.

Page 102

Perhaps one of the strongest arguments for the process of natural selection is that we can mimic it using **artificial** selection. As mentioned

earlier, the first chapter in Darwin's *Origin of the Species* is "Variation Under Domestication," and it deals with the process of picking and choosing who breeds with whom. The plasticity of domesticated organisms subjected to artificial selection is evident when he notes that "[o]ur oldest cultivated plants, such as wheat, still yield new varieties: our oldest domesticated animals are still capable of rapid improvement or modification."

Chapter 5
Legacy

Page 109

The persecution of radical thinkers was common in Darwin's day. As a student at Cambridge, Darwin saw individuals who challenged social and clerical orthodoxy jailed or punished in some other way. In one case, a landlord and father of six had his housing license revoked for no other reason than renting a room to a freethinking radical. All of this was within the bounds of the prevailing heresy and sedition laws.

Numerous similar incidents helped contribute to Darwin's own fear about his ideas and his reluctance to publish them. He knew full well that many of his compatriots might turn on him because of his views, and he did not want to lose his respectability and social standing. He certainly didn't want to be publicly hounded and humiliated.

In fact, Darwin was cautious and secretive about his theory for many years before he published the *Origin of the Species*. And even then, he only did so because he was afraid he was going to be scooped. So imagine

Darwin's horror when, after 20 years of hard work, specimen collecting and experimentation, he received a letter from a young naturalist named Alfred Russell Wallace that proposed an evolutionary mechanism similar to natural selection. Wallace had actually been corresponding with Darwin for some time before he sent the fateful letter of June 18, 1858. He conceived his evolutionary theory while under the feverish sway of malaria in the Spice Islands. He wrote it up and asked Darwin to pass it along to Charles Lyell for publication. Darwin was bummed!

Alfred Russel Wallace

Fortunately, Darwin's work wasn't completely closeted. He had confided in his friends Charles Lyell and Joseph Hooker. (He said that when he told Hooker about natural selection, he felt like he was confessing to murder.) Lyell had actually encouraged to him to publish much earlier so he wouldn't be scooped, and Hooker was giving Darwin feedback on his *Natural Selection* manuscript.

Naturally, Darwin wanted credit for his work. Who could blame him? But he didn't want it to seem as if he were stealing Wallace's idea. He was in a tough situation and Hooker and

Lyell helped him out. They arranged for him to present his theory jointly with Wallace's at a meeting of the Linnaean Society in 1858. He completed the *Origin of the Species* the next year.

Joseph Hooker

Page 115
One of the most startling (and hazardous) things about myths is that they sometimes touch lightly on reality. Aside from the metaphysical elements of Flycatcher extracting a fiber of being from each parent, there is something in this myth that isn't quite right.

I'm trying to be clever when I have Flycatcher twist those fibers of being into the familiar looking double helix of DNA. However, I feel compelled to point out that combining one strand from the mother and one strand from the father does NOT make DNA. As mentioned earlier, our genome, or genetic make up, consists of 23 pairs of chromosomes (chromosomes are the molecules upon which genes are found). We get one member of each pair from our mom and one from our dad. Each chromosome is a double-strand. So, everything we get from each parent is double stranded.

Page 117, Panel 1

There were four primary objections leveled at Darwinian Natural Selection by its opponents: 1) that the Earth was not old enough for gradual evolutionary change to occur (Lord Kelvin's contention), 2) that incipient organs could never lead to more complex structures like a wing (Mivart's contention), 3) the absence of intermediate types in the fossil record and 4) Darwin's inability to explain a mechanism for inheritance.

We have addressed the first two points earlier in the story and annotations, so we can address the second two now. First, let's consider the lack of intermediates in the fossil record.

Darwin believed that evolutionary change occurred gradually over great stretches of time. His critics contended that if this were the case, we should see a multitude of gradually changing intermediate animal forms in the fossil record. We don't. To some, this lack of intermediates seemed like a pretty compelling argument against gradualism and, by extension, Darwinism. Compelling, of course, until you consider a few basic facts.

First, there are very specific conditions required for fossilization. You usually need to die in the water (80-90% of all known fossil organisms are aquatic). Once dead in the water (I couldn't resist), an organism needs to be deposited someplace where it can be covered quickly in mud or sand before its bones are scattered by scavengers. River bends and sea or lake bottoms are usually good for this. Then it has to lie there undisturbed and wait for its bones to be turned slowly to rock by the sediment. Now, this process alone has obviously biased the fossil record dramatically toward aquatic forms. Add to that the fact that paleontologists can't find all of the fossil needles in our earthly haystack, and we are bound to have a woefully incomplete fossil record. One text suggests that the several hundred thousand fossil species so far identified represent only 0.001% of all the species that have ever existed!

The other problem with demanding fossil intermediates is the resolution of the geological record. Most paleontologists believe that the fossil record is only reliable down to a resolution of about a million years. So, from a paleontologist's perspective, when something happens in less than a million years, it is effectively "instantaneous" in the fossil record. Of course, from an evolutionary biologist standpoint, a million years is plenty of time for big changes to occur.

Add to all of this the debate over the rate of evolutionary change. Was it gradual? Or do periods of rapid species change punctuate long periods of relative stability or equilibrium? Niles Eldredge and Stephen Jay Gould proposed this theory of punctuated equilibrium in 1972. The debate that followed was vigorous, but a recent review of the literature by Erwin and Anstney (1995 a, b) suggests that there is evidence that both punctuated equilibrium and gradualism have played a role in evolution.

Some anti-evolutionists have seized upon these debates as evidence that science can't agree on evolution. This, of course, is a misrepresentation. These debates focus on the details of *how* evolution has occurred, not *if* it occurred. No theory in science is known absolutely and evolution is no different.

Now, let's consider the fourth objection. The inability to explain inheritance dogged Darwin. To work, natural selection needs inherited characteristics to be discrete so that they can be 1) acted upon by natural selection and 2) passed completely to the next generation. At the time, the prevailing theory of heredity was that parental characteristics "blended" together in their children. In this theory, an advantageous trait would soon be diluted over time by breeding with members of the population that lack the trait.

Darwin developed his own theory of heredity called Pangenesis and, well, I'll let him explain it: "...each cell [of the body] throws off an atom of its content or a gemmule, and that these, aggregated [to] form the true ovule or bud." So, each part of the body sends a bit of itself as a representative to the reproductive organs. In the end, this explanation didn't work. Two of Darwin's supporters, Francis Galton and George Romanes, failed to find experimental evidence to support Pangenesis and the theory was eventually abandoned.

In the face of the criticisms listed above, Darwinism fell from favor in the late 19th century and continued to be out of vogue well into the 20th century. While most scientists accepted the fact of evolution, mechanisms more palatable than natural selection were in fashion. Specifically, many favored the idea that a supernatural Creator guided evolution. It wasn't until the birth of modern genetics and the formulation of the Modern Synthesis (mentioned in the annotations for Chapter 3) that natural selection truly came back into its own.

Panel 2
Darwin displays an astonishing bit of prescience here. This "imagined" quotation from future historians is, in fact, on page 642 of *Darwin: The Life of a Tormented Evolutionist* by Desmond and Moore.

Panel 10
One of the hallmarks of anti-evolution arguments is that since the theory is incomplete, it must be wrong. But a theory is only ever the best explanation possible given the evidence at hand. There is no requirement that it be complete. In fact, one might ask how completeness could be ascertained. How many fossil species will we have to collect for the fossil record to be "complete?" Obviously, this is an impossible proposition. But does anyone dispute that dinosaurs once roamed the earth, just because we haven't "completed" the fossil record? Natural selection has withstood almost 150 years of intensive scrutiny from scientists, clergy and laypeople. After years of dissection and public debate, it remains the best explanation for the process of evolution

Page 118, Panel 8
Darwin lost his mother when he was 8 years old. By his own admission, he remembers very little about her. In his autobiography, he can describe her black funeral dress and medicine table, but very little else. It is safe to say that it was probably a pretty traumatic event for an 8 year old. He also suggests that his older sisters' unwillingness to discuss their

mother and his mother's invalid state may have further contributed to his dearth of memories.

Page 119

Darwin lost three children in his lifetime: Annie (1841-1851), Mary Eleanor (1842) and Charles Waring (1856-1858). By most accounts, the rest of his children were somewhat sickly in nature. Most biographers, including his son Francis, paint Darwin as a devoted and doting father. So, it must have been very difficult for him to see his children suffer with weak constitutions that were probably inherited from him.

Panel 6

I have been informed by a number of people I've met that we are not meant to know certain things. I am always struck by the historical context of this type of statement. Were we "meant" to know that the Earth wasn't the center of the universe? I'll bet some of Galileo's critics didn't think we should know. He was excommunicated for his ideas, after all. These days everybody except members of The Flat Earth Society are comfortable with the idea that the earth sits on the periphery of the Milky Way galaxy a long, long way from the center of the universe. I've tried to underscore this historical context by using the heredity example in this story. Daunting as heredity must have seemed to Darwin and his contemporaries, these days most of us are just as comfortable with the notion of genes as the units of heredity as we are with the position of our planet in space.

In the end, there was no metaphysical barrier standing between genes and our understanding. This discovery was waiting for the right bit of technology, as well as the right cultural and intellectual climate.

Panel 8

I cannot leave this topic without mentioning one interesting historical note. The father of modern genetics was a Moravian monk named Gregor Mendel (1822 - 1884). Mendel's experiments with pea plants furnished the first mathematical evidence that the units of heredity are discrete. Unfortunately, his work wasn't appreciated for what it was in his time, and it was only rediscovered in the early 20th century.

Gregor Mendel

Mendel and Darwin were contemporaries, but Mendel toiled away in relative obscurity. He knew of Charles Darwin, though. After Darwin's death, an unopened copy of Mendel's paper was found in his library. It is one of those tantalizing stories of almost discovery that pinches the imagination. But, as Robin Marantz Henig points out in her book *The Monk in the Garden*, there is no guarantee, given his weak mathematical skills, that Darwin would have appreciated Mendel's work for what it was, even if he had read it.

Page 120

Bernard Darwin was the son of Emma and Charles' son Francis. Bernard's nickname was Abbadubba, and Charles often complained of not getting to spend enough time with him.

Francis Darwin

Francis collaborated with his father on many projects when they lived together and eventually became a lecturer in Botany at Cambridge. I have Bernard find a leaf as a nod to his father Francis' area of expertise. Sir Francis Darwin was knighted in 1913.

Page 121

The comment in the fourth panel is my invention. But, from what I have read of Emma, it feels like something she would have said to remind Charles of what's important. The remark can have an evolutionary context, as well. What *is* more important in an evolutionary sense than the children you leave? Of course, that is clearly not what a Unitarian fundamentalist like Emma would have meant if she had said it.

Page 125

As was the case with the walking stick, I didn't find proper reference for Darwin's microscope until after the fifth chapter was at the printer. I

received the second volume of Janet Browne's biography of Darwin (*Charles Darwin: The Power of Place*) for my birthday and let out a healthy "GAH!" as I flipped through the illustrations and saw the microscope Darwin favored. I have redrawn the offending panel for this book and present the original panel here for your consideration.

Page 126

At 3 pm, Emma or one of Charles' daughters would read him a novel while he relaxed and dozed

Page 127, Panel 3

Charles didn't take losing at backgammon well. He and Emma kept a running tally of their several hundred games. Although he led in the overall tally, if he was trailing he would often exclaim in exasperation to Emma, "bang your bones!"

Panel 5

As Mara reaches desperately for Bernard's head, I couldn't resist the Sistine Chapel visual reference. Who could?

Bibliography

Atkins KBE, Sir Hedley. 1974. *Down: The Home of the Darwins.* Phillimore

Barlow, Nora, editor. 1969. *The Autobiography of Charles Darwin.* New York: W. W. Norton & Company.

Barrett, Paul H., editor. 1977. *The Collected Papers of Charles Darwin.* The University of Chicago Press.

Borror, Donald J., Thriplehorn, Charles A. and Johnson, Norman F. 1989. *An Introduction to Insects.* 6th ed. New York: Harcourt Brace College Publishers

Bowlby, John. 1990. *Charles Darwin, A New Life.* New York: W. W. Norton & Company.

Browne, Janet. 1995. *Charles Darwin, Voyaging.* Princeton University Press.

___. 2002. *Charles Darwin, The Power of Place.* Alfred A. Knopf, New York

Burkhardt, Frederick, editor. 1996. *Charles Darwin's Letters, A Selection,* Cambridge University Press.

Cambell, Joseph. 1949. *The Hero with a Thousand Faces.* Bollingen Series XVII, Princeton University Press

Chancellor, John. 1973. *Charles Darwin.* New York: Taplinger Publishing Co., Inc.

Conniff, Richard. 1998. Body Beasts. *National Geographic Magazine.* December

Darwin, Charles. 1989. *Voyage of the Beagle.* Penguin Books (originally published in 1839 by Henry Colburn).

___.1993. *The Origin of Species.* The Modern Library Edition.

___.1998. *The Expressions of the Emotions in Man and Animals.* 3rd ed. Oxford University Press.

___.editor. 1841. *The Zoology of the Voyage of HMS Beagle.*

Dawkins, Richard. 1996. *Climbing Mount Improbable.* New York: W.W. Norton & Company

Desmond, Adrian J., and Moore, James. 1991. *Darwin, The Life of a Tormented Evolutionist.* New York: W. W. Norton & Company.

Freemon, Scott and Herron, Jon C. 2001. *Evolutionary Analysis.* 2nd ed. Prentice Hall.

Gamlin, Linda. 1993. *Evolution.* London: Dorling Kindersley.

Gould, Stephen Jay and Vrba, Elisabeth S. 1982. Exaptation-a missing term in the science of form. *Paleobiology*, **8**: 1, pp. 4-15.

Gould, Stephen Jay. 1991. Not Necessarily a Wing. In *Bully for Brontosaurus*, 139-151. New York: W. W. Norton & Company.

Gould, Stephen Jay, editor. 1993. *The Book of Life.* New York: W. W. Norton & Company.

Henig, Robin Marantz. 2000. *The Monk in the Garden.* Houghton Mifflin Co.

Huxley, Julian and Kettlewell, H.B.D. 1965. *Darwin and His World.* New York: The Viking Press.

Kingsolver, Joel G. and Koehl, M. A. R. 1985. Aerodynamics, thermoregulation, and the evolution of insect wings: differential scaling and evolutionary change. *Evolution* **39**: 3, pp 488-504.

Landau, Misia. 1991. *Naratives of Human Evolution.* New Haven, CT: Yale University Press.

Larson, Edward J. 1997. *Summer of the Gods: The Scopes Trial and America's Continuing Debate over Science and Religion.* New York: Basic Books.

Lightbinders. 2001. *Darwin 2nd Edition CD-ROM,* The Complete Works of Charles Darwin.

Marden, James H. and Kramer, Melissa G. 1994. Surface-Skimming Stoneflies: A possible Intermediate Stage in Insect Flight Evolution. *Science* **266**: 5184. pp 427-430.

Marden, James H., O'Donnel, Brigid C., Thomas, Michael A. and Bye, Jesse Y. 2000. Surface-Skimming Stoneflies and Mayflies: The taxonomic and Mechanical Diversity of Two-Dimensional Aerodynamic Locomotion, *Physiol. and Biochem Zool.* **73**: 6, 751-764

Mayr, Ernst. 1982. *The Growth of Biological Thought: Diversity, Evolution aand Inheritance.* Cambridge, MA: Harvard University Press.

___.2001. *What Evolution Is.* New York: Basic Books.

Miller, Jonathan and Van Loon, Borin. 1982. *Darwin for Beginners.* Pantheon Books.

Milner, Richard. 1990. *The Encyclopedia of Evolution.* New York: Henry Holt and Company

Moore, James. 1994. *The Darwin Legend.* Baker Books.

Moorehead, Alan. 1969. *Darwin and the Beagle.* Harper & Row.

Norman, David and Milner, Angela. 1989. *Dinosaur.* New York: Alfred A, Knopf.

Pennock, Robert T. 2002. *Tower of Babel: The Evidence against the New Creationism.* Cambridge, MA: MIT Press.

Weiner, Jonathan. 1994. *The Beak of the Finch.* New York: Vintage Books.

Will, Kipling W., Marden, James H. and Kramer, Melissa G. 1995. Plecoptera Surface-Skimming and Insect Flight Evolution, *Science,* **207**: 5242, pp 1684-1685

Zimmer, Carl. 2001. *Evolution.* Harper Collins Publishers

Acknowledgements

First and foremost, I thank my wife, **Lisa,** for copyediting, helping with the logo, reading and commenting on initial drafts, providing advice on artistic direction and helping with cover colors. Anyone who knows me knows what a sap I am about my wife. She is my best friend and the frontline for all of my creative endeavors. Lisa holds my feet to the fire and never lets me settle for "good enough." The truth is, I'm stubborn and don't always take criticism that well. Fortunately for my books, Lisa is more stubborn, and most of my objections to her criticism spring from laziness more than anything else. Thanks, Lisa Suzanne Guerra Hosler.

My eldest son, **Max,** helped with the erasing on several pages and often held the ruler for me as I inked panel borders. He also modeled for the tongue-rolling picture.

Laura and **Jamie White** were eagle-eyed editors and took me to the woodshed for my numerous grammatical errors. Thankfully, the errors were never so bad that they felt compelled to take me to their compost heap.

Thanks to the indefatigable **Daryn Guarino** for performing the Herculean task of doing all the annoying business things that would be done much more slowly (and poorly) if I had to do them. It is a massive endeavor, and Daryn's tireless advocacy and promotion of this book and my first book, *Clan Apis,* have been crucial for finding an audience. Especially since he's the guy that mails them out!

Discussions with **Gib Bickel, Jeff Mara, Sally Oberle, John Matter, Rachel Hartman, Carle Speed McNeil, Randy Bennett, Doug Glazier, Vince Buonocorrsi, Jill Keeney, Ryan Mathur, Jim Ottaviani, Sandy McBride, Dave Hsiung, Belle Tuten, Jim Tuten** and **Harry Itagaki** were invaluable at various stages in the ...uh...*evolution* of this story. Talking with these folks helped me to clarify, expand or correct my thoughts on evolution, natural selection, genetics, geology, history and pedagogy. The only thing that fuels my creative process as much as reading is talking with interesting people about interesting things.

I especially appreciate my lively discussion with **John Wenzel** at Ohio State University about the evolution of insect flight. I was a bit stuck on where to go with Chapter 4, and talking with John was like a creative enema. Hmm, I probably should work on that metaphor...

I also appreciate the work of **David Leff,** whose *AboutDarwin.com* has been an excellent source for visual reference.

Special thanks to my colleague **Nancy Siegel** at the Juniata College Museum of Art for helping me get a drawing board for my office. Kudos to **Jeremy Santos** and **Kathryn Oser** at the Juniata College Bookstore for helping me find art supplies.

Thanks to **Zander Cannon** for convincing me to hand letter this book and **John Kerschbaum** for the Darwin illustrations that now adorn my office wall.

Thanks to **Kim Preney, Kevin Johnson** and all of the fine folks at **Preney Print and Litho** for the excellent work.

Finally, thanks to my family, for all of their support in everything I do.

ABOUT THE AUTHOR

Jay Hosler is an Assistant Professor of Biology at Juniata College, where he teaches Neurobiology and Invertebrate Biology. His research focuses on learning and sensory biology and has been published in the *Journal of Experimental Biology, Behavioral Neuroscience* and *The Journal of Insect Physiology*. A doodler from birth, he began writing cartoons as an undergraduate at DePauw University, where his strip *Under the Bubble* ran for three years in *The DePauw*. In graduate school at the University of Notre Dame, his strip *Spelunker* ran for five years in *The Observer,* while he worked on his doctoral research on the effect of temperature on insect flight muscle electrophysiology. After receiving his degree, he moved on to Ohio State University's Rothenbuhler Honey Bee Research Laboratory, where his postdoctoral research on honey bee odor learning was funded by a grant from the National Institutes of Health. It was in Columbus that he got the big idea to combine his love of science and cartooning to make comic books. His first graphic novel, *Clan Apis*, is the biography of a honey bee and has been awarded a Xeric Award, nominated for 5 Eisner Awards and 3 Ignatz Awards and named to the Young Adult Library Services Association 25 Best Graphic Novels for 2002. Dr. Hosler lives in central PA with his wife, Lisa, and sons Max and Jack. When he isn't writing self-aggrandizing "About the Author" sections in an attempt to give himself an air of legitimacy, he can be found rolling around the floor with his boys and making goo-goo eyes at his wife.